BELLAMI UNDERWOOD

The Baddest BOOK FINAL

First edition

This book was professionally typeset on Reedsy.
Find out more at reedsy.com

Contents

Introduction

The Baddest

By Bellami Underwood

By Bellami Underwood

For the ones they counted out.

For the dreamers who didn't know what came next, but still kept pushing.

This book is for the survivors, the soft hearts, the loud souls, and the quiet warriors.

It's for anyone who ever felt lost, scared, unseen — but showed up anyway.

Your scars don't define you — they refine you.

You're not broken, you're becoming.

This is for you.

Foreword

To my supporters — my Brista fam,

Never did I imagine I'd be writing a book. And not just any book — a book that holds my heart,

my imagination, my vulnerability. There was a time I didn't know who I was or where I was going.

But through storytelling, I found healing. I found me.

The Baddest is fiction — but every emotion inside it is real. These stories are layered. Raw. Human.

Whether you've lived this life or loved someone who has, I know you'll relate.

I hope while reading, you give yourself permission to explore. To cry. To laugh. To heal.

And to know this: no matter how dark things get, there's always light waiting for you at the end.

With love & light,

Bellami Underwood

Imagine being the baddest in every room you walk into. Not just cute — that girl.

12th grade. Senior year. Graduation around the corner. Life finally starting to look like something.

Coming up in a single-parent home after your mom and dad split early, you always felt like you had to fend for yourself.

Your older brother too busy running the streets, your sister barely around — and even when they were, it's like they never saw you.

But the streets did.

The streets always saw me.

I'm Indyanna. A pretty girl from Frankford with a passion for fashion, a hustle in her step, and a heart that beat louder than most.

Between cheer practice, fashion shows, the nursing program, and barely keeping my lil bootleg car from getting booted again, I was on a mission.

Nobody could say I wasn't trying to level up. My plate stayed full — but one thing about me? I'ma eat.

And right by my side? My girl TeeTee. Short for Teyana.

We was raised on hood nicknames and hot combs. She been my day one since middle school — loud, loyal, and just as ghetto fabulous as me.

"Sisterhood" don't even cut it. That's my twin flame in a bonnet.

At least, that's what I thought...

So boom — this all starts right after I broke it off with my ex, Kev.

Three whole years wasted. From fighting uptown bitches who swore they had one up on me, to finding out he had a baby on the way — he put me through it.

I knew I had to let him go, and not just for my peace... but for my future.

Kev was dead weight. He was slowing me down, and I had places to be.

The morning after one of those long nights — studying, doing my hair, planning outfits, trying to manifest a better life — I woke up late.

I didn't even have time to roll my edges right. My car? Broke down. Boot list. Ghetto.

So I called an Ubi and slid to school praying I'd make it in time.

I did. Barely. Hit my classes, linked with Tee on lunch, but I already knew I had to stay after for my internship.

Nursing program — shout out to Ms. Patrica — she don't play about me.

But I ain't gon' lie... I didn't know nothing on that test.

So I leaned over to this girl Anita and hit her with the "sis, help me cheat" eyes.

And yup — I cheated. And passed.

After the program, I checked my phone.

Ubi prices? Through the roof.

I thought about calling Kev — but nah. I had too much pride.

So I hopped on the bus like a real one.

What I didn't expect... was to run into him.

Daul.

My brother's friend.

Street nigga. Trap nigga. *That* nigga.

Fine as hell. Chocolate. Tatted. Smelling like Dior Sauvage and decisions.

The type of man who had a past, a lil mystery, and a whole lot of "lemme see what this about."

He seen me stepping off the bus and started honking, yelling out the window like, "Yo! You don't hear me calling you?"

I lied like I was deep in my music. Embarrassed as hell.

But he didn't care. He parked the car and started walking with me.

I ain't gon' lie, I used to hear about Daul.

That he messed with girls from my school. Had a couple kids. Sold weight. Ran the block.

But standing next to him? All that melted.

He was calm. Gentle even.

And when he said, "You hungry? Let's go to Haneefah's," I played hard to get.

But I was starving. So I said yes.

We sat. We ate. He talked.

And it was something about the way he talked...

He wasn't dumb. He had vision.

Talkin' 'bout buying property, getting out the game, flipping his money legit.

Most dudes his age couldn't see past the next party.

But Daul? He was talking legacy. Ownership.

I was listening — but also staring at his lips, wondering how he still had baby-soft skin with all that stress.

Meanwhile, Tee kept blowing up my phone like a pressed auntie.

I sent her a pic like, "Girl, I'm with my man!"

She hit me back with a voice memo laughing, like, "Bitch, we gotta talk."

Anyway, Daul and I chilled for a while. Then he said, "Let's go for a walk."

Why did my dumbass end up at his house?

I ain't even have a stay-the-night bag. I ain't even shave my legs like that.

But when we got there... listen.

I was expecting trap house.

I walked into a downtown loft.

Minimalist. Clean. Organized.

Books on the shelf. A vinyl player in the corner.

He had incense burning.

I was like — who is this man?

Next thing you know, we was in the sheets.

Don't ask how. Don't ask why. Just know it happened.

And baby... it was good.

Like... scary good.

Like, "What's your zodiac sign again?" good.

He had me out here ready to risk it all.

Tall. Solid. Clean nails. Fresh fade. Dreamy eyes. And respect on his breath.

When I tell you I don't normally do stuff like that? I mean it.

But something about Daul made me feel safe and seen.

And stupid.

The next morning, he dropped me off at school.

Gave me hush money and a forehead kiss. I was cheesin'.

Tee seen me and said, "That ain't no Ubi."

I told her, "Mind ya business." And then I told her everything.

Later that day, this man sent me food — sushi and fries. *At school.* In front of everybody.

I was like, Daul, you trying to get me jumped?

These girls already side-eyeing me, knowing they used to mess with you.

But Tee? She hyped me up.

"That's your man. This your moment. *Period.*"

And that's how he became mine.

Chapter Two

The Baddest – Chapter Two

By Bellami Underwood

Weeks flew by, and at this point, me and my man?

We was basically conjoined.

Every night I was out, and every time I came home, my mom hit me with the same question:

Why you **always gone? You live here or nah?**

I'd lie with a straight face.

Ma, it's senior year — cheer, school, helping Tee out. I'm busy.

Whole time?

I was ridin' Daul like a borrowed bike with no brakes.

But she ain't need to know all that.

That morning, I got up for school and something felt... off.

Not in my body.

In my *spirit.*

My intuition was tapping me on the shoulder like:

You sure **Tee really happy for you?**

Ever since I got with Daul, she'd been acting different.

Less calls. Canceled plans. Distant.

I figured she just missed our girl time, so when I saw her at school, I brought it up.

You **good?** You been **weird.**

I been busy, she shrugged, then added,

You the **one with a man now.**

I laughed.

Yup. Now I just gotta get you one.

She fake laughed with me, but the smile didn't reach her eyes.

I ignored it.

I didn't want to believe what I was starting to feel.

Later in class, my stomach wouldn't stop flipping.

I couldn't focus.

I dipped out to the bathroom twice, then headed to the Women's Center.

I called Tee to meet me.

When she got there, I told the nurse my symptoms, and they had me take a test.

Y'all...

I was pregnant.

I damn near blacked out in the chair.

I just kept whispering,

No. No. No. This can't be.

Tee, loud as ever, said:

Girl, F them kids! Get an abortion and get back to life.

Her words hit me like ice water... but a part of me needed it.

I was spiraling.

I hadn't told nobody — not my mom, not Daul, and definitely not my brother.

And since Daul was his friend?

Whew.

Tee said,

Let's focus on telling Daul first.

After school, I skipped my internship and had him come pick me up.

We pulled up at Haneefah's.

Sat down.

I didn't wait for the food.

I'm pregnant.

He blinked.

Stop playin'.

Don't play in my face, Daul.

He smirked.

Who baby? Ain't mine.

SMACK.

He laughed.

Damn, chill — I'm jokin'. Forreal?

I nodded.

He reached across the table, rubbed my stomach and said:

Aww shit. I'm 'bout to be a dad.

My heart softened.

I told him I wasn't sure about keeping it.

I was supposed to graduate. Go off to college. Live my life.

But that man? He had a way with words.

He told me he'd support me. Raise the baby. Build a future.

I started to believe in the fantasy.

Hell, I even felt a little excited.

That night, I told my mom.

I brought him to the house, all nervous.

She opened the door, gave him one look and said:

So this the **reason** you been **gone every night? Lemme guess — y'all f**kin.**

MOM! I screamed.

She wasn't wrong.

I told her I was pregnant.

She blinked, laughed, and said:

I knew it! You wasn't **at no Tee house — you** was **gettin' that box hot and ready!**

Even Daul laughed.

Yo, your mom crazy.

But she accepted me,

That's what matters.

I decided not to leave for school.

Me and Daul talked it through.

He was stepping up.

Really being *that* man.

And I was falling in love.

Not just with him — but with the idea of *us*.

We planned the gender reveal — big "Him or Her" theme, with a package dropping from the sky and fireworks exploding the color.

When that blue smoke shot into the air?

I smiled through my tears.

A baby boy.

A little prince.

A king in the making.

Tee came through, hyped like old times.

Brought her new man. Acted like nothing had changed.

My brother was back in town helping me plan the baby shower.

And even Kimmy — always-hatin' sister — showed up.

We hadn't spoken in months.

She always swore I wanted her life.

Like I'd ever want to be a stay-at-home punching bag for a man who beat her, bought her silence, and fed her lies.

But she came. Showed out. Bought half my registry.

The baby shower was magic.

Pink and blue flowers everywhere. Intimate vibes. Plates full of soul food.

Why Don't We Fall in Love by Amerie playing in the background.

My whole family line-dancing in the living room.

For once, I felt *seen.*

After the party, I went to my mom's to pack some things before heading to Daul's.

Tee offered to help him unload the U-Haul.

I said thank you — not knowing what she was really unloading.

Because while I was hugging my mama goodbye...

My baby daddy was fking my best friend in the back of a truck.**

I didn't know.

Not yet.

I got to his house late that night.

He was fresh out the shower.

I thought nothing of it — figured he wanted to be clean before cuddling up.

But then I saw Tee's jewelry on the bed.

Why is her stuff in my room? I asked.

He blinked.

Oh, she just dropped it when we were moving.

My gut twisted.

We argued.

But he was good.

Too good.

He manipulated. Gaslit. Smoothed it all over.

I let it go.

Focused on the baby.

On nesting.

On our future.

Monday came.

Movers arrived.

We moved into our new place — a gorgeous 3-bedroom townhouse.

I wanted to feel safe, so I installed cameras.

Called Daul to get the login.

Logged in. Synced everything to my phone.

What I didn't know?

The system backed up all his past footage.

Every file.

Every date.

Every moment.

Out of curiosity, I scrolled back to the day of my baby shower.

I wanted to see how happy we looked.

I didn't see sex.

I saw Tee helping with boxes.

I felt relief. Like, *okay cool — maybe I'm just paranoid.*

But something told me: **keep watching.**

Then I saw my brother.

Over and over.

Pulling up.

Leaving.

Returning.

Again.

And again.

Then... I saw it.

A hug.

A kiss.

Then more.

My baby daddy. And my brother. Having sex.

Tears fell before I could even scream.

I kept scrolling.

Watching.

Confirming.

It wasn't just once.

It was a pattern.

I blacked out.

Threw the phone. Smashed mirrors. Burned shoes. Flipped the crib.

I was in full-blown rage mode.

Then my water broke.

Blood on my hands. Cuts on my arms. Screams that didn't sound human.

The neighbors thought someone was dying.

And they were right.

It was me.

The EMTs came.

Asked for my emergency contact.

I gave them his number.

They called him.

And I cursed him the **ENTIRE** way to the hospital.

Emergency C-section.

My body sliced open for a child I no longer wanted.

I birthed my son numb.

In recovery, I looked up and saw them all — Tee, Daul, his mother, my brother.

Laughing.

Celebrating.

Like nothing happened.

I couldn't hold it in.

I told the room everything.

The cheating. The betrayal. The videos. The baby.

Tee swung on Daul.

I thought she was fighting for me.

Nah — she was fighting her baby daddy too.

Yup.

We were both pregnant by the same man.

A man who was also sleeping with my brother.

This wasn't just betrayal.

It was war.

I kicked everyone out.

Called my dad.

He answered on the second ring.

Indy? You okay?

I couldn't even speak. Just sobbed into the phone until I could get the words out.

Daddy... I can't do this. I can't be here. I need you.

That man didn't ask questions.

He didn't lecture me.

He didn't judge me.

He just said:

Pack your things. I'm on my way.

He drove all night from Georgia.

Eight hours.

No sleep.

Barely stopped to pee.

And when he walked into that hospital room the next morning and saw me —

Swollen eyes. Fresh stitches. Barely breathing through the pain —

He held me like I was five years old again.

You don't ever have to go through nothing like this alone again, you hear me? he whispered.

I nodded into his chest, finally feeling like somebody was really on my side.

I'll handle everything, he said.

The adoption. The paperwork. The hospital. Your things. I just need you to rest now.

For the first time in what felt like forever, I exhaled.

My father made the arrangements with the social worker.
Found the family.
Read through every line of every form.
And when I told him I didn't want the baby to know who I was — at least not right now — he nodded.
No pushback.
Just protection.

That man was my anchor in a storm that tried to drown me.
With his help, I signed the papers.
Kissed my baby boy's forehead.
Whispered a prayer.
And let go.

A beautiful family in the South adopted him.
I asked for no name. No visits.
Just contact in case I ever changed my mind.

Then I packed what was left of me and moved to Georgia with my dad.
I left Philly behind.

From Philly cheesesteaks to Georgia peaches...
I became something new.

Chapter Three

The Baddest – Chapter Three

By Bellami Underwood

Going to Georgia?

Man, I never imagined this would be my life.

Are you fucking kidding me?

I'm a Philly girl.

Why am I now driving 12 hours across states with my dad, my bags, and my tears — leaving behind a baby I barely got to hold, with a family I don't even know?

I ain't even get the chance to enjoy my new life.

Now here I am, starting over... again.

I sat in that car, pretending to sleep, pretending to be fine, but my thoughts were loud.

Loud like the city I just left.

I was prepping myself for the unknown: postpartum, a new body I didn't recognize, these big-ass titties that popped up like surprise guests.

I had to relearn who I was.

Again.

We pulled into Georgia, and baby, I knew I wasn't in Philly no more.

I smelled fried chicken, red clay, thirsty bugs, and opportunity.

Something about the air told me,

This is your reset.

So I made a decision:

I was gonna fix everything I fumbled.

Period.

A few weeks in, I felt stuck — until I remembered something: my email.

I checked it, and boom.

A southern HBCU had reached out, still holding a spot for me.

I showed it to my dad, told him,

"I think I'm ready to float again. I'm ready to not let my past define my future."

He gave me that look — nervous but proud — and said I had to talk to my brother first.

I hesitated, but I did it.

When my brother flew in, he dropped a bomb.

Told me my baby daddy had been out here messing with dudes, going to gay after-hours, getting passed around like free samples.

I was shocked but not surprised.

I knew my brother wouldn't lie.

We made a pact right there:

Let the past be the past.

The next day, we drove to the school.

My brother stayed in the car because I said so — I wasn't letting his energy fumble my restart.

I registered for classes, did a walk-through, and baby, when I say the southern men?

They was built different.

Fine. Respectful. Sexy.

That's when I met DJ.

Brown skin, pretty smile, body on natural athlete.

He was my campus tour guide.

Said he played football, loved his family, and just wanted to be the best version of himself.

I was lowkey blushing but tried to keep it cute.

"Y'all got sororities?" I asked.

He smiled,

"Yeah, my cousin Jessica could put you on game."

Jessica.

Whew.

When I found her, I instantly knew she was that girl.

Dark skin, bright red hair, body like she walked out a music video.

She had that "I run this campus" energy.

She was expecting me too — DJ had already put her on.

She hugged me like we been cool.

Told me to pull up to a Who's Who party that night.

So I did.

I threw on a maxi dress, heels, and a cute lil cropped jacket.

When I walked in with Jessica, I felt like a celebrity.

Everybody turned.

Tamika, one of the other girls, greeted me like she already loved me.

Girls' girl energy — instantly one of my favorites.

Then guess who I spotted?

DJ.

Looking edible with his boys.

I whispered to Jessica,

"That's my man."

She laughed,

"Girl, everybody want **DJ, but can't nobody** keep **him. But... he is staring at you hard, so maybe you got a chance."**

He walked over.

We talked.

Flirted.

Vibes were crazy.

You could feel the hateration from the other girls, but I didn't care.

This was my moment.

DJ asked if I stayed on campus.

I said I wasn't sure yet.

Then he hit me with,

"You want me to take you home?"

Before I could answer, loud-ass Jessica jumped in:

"Not tonight!"

I laughed.

"Damn, okay!"

We left the party.

Jess dropped me off, grilled me with a million questions, and I spilled everything.

The next few days flew by.

I met more people.

Me and my BRISTA bonded instantly.

We were inseparable.

When homecoming rolled around, we decided to go all out — new outfits, makeup, energy.

I was excited to see DJ play.

Number 7.

He was killin' it.

But while we were cheering him on, I peeped someone on the other team.

Tall. Cocky. Confident.

After the game, he walked straight up to me.

"You. Come here."

I was like,

Who, me?

Innocent face on.

Guilty thoughts spinning.

He asked for my number.

DJ was watching.

I felt it.

My BRISTA gave me the look like,

"Girl... he watching**!"**

So I made it quick and handed over the number.

Jessica pulled me away — only to run into DJ.

"That your **man?"** he asked.

I lied.

"He from **Philly. Mind your business."**

DJ smirked.

"Don't make me turn this game into a funeral."

Whew. Pressure.

Then he softened.

"You **hungry?"**

We pulled up to a chicken and waffle spot — same place as before.

DJ was tearing up his plate like he hadn't eaten in days, but I didn't judge.

We talked.

Laughed.

Cuddled in the booth like we were already something.

That's when it happened — the kiss.

Soft.

Sweet.

Syrup still on his breath.

It was giving everything.

Then he looked at me like he had something serious to say.

"Come stay with me tonight."

And I wanted to.

Every part of me said yes.

But my spirit tapped me on the shoulder and said,

Don't forget who you are.

So I told him no.

He respected it.

Instead, he smiled and said,

"My family's having a party tomorrow. Welcoming a new kid we adopted. Come with me. Dress cute. Look **like pressure."**

"Jessica coming?" I asked.

He laughed.

"Duh. That's my cousin."

I nodded, biting back my smile.

"Bet."

That night, I went to sleep thinking about what I was gonna wear.

Not just for the party... but for the new life I was stepping into.

Because something told me — **this was only the beginning.**

Chapter Four

The Baddest – Chapter Four

By Bellami Underwood

Something in my spirit told me the day was gonna be messy.

I was getting dressed for the event like everything was normal, but my intuition?

Loud.

Jessica pulled up, blasting music, big smile on her face like we was headed to just another bougie get-together.

I had no clue DJ was rich rich.

I'm talkin' big-ass house, gated community, fancy-ass cars in the driveway.

His family?

Pretty, polished, paid.

We mingling, chillin' — me, Jessica, Tamika, my BRISTA — until DJ spots us and pulls me in with that signature grin.

"Come meet my family," he said.

Everyone was cool — except one slick-mouthed chick named Shantel.

"She always **rude,"** DJ whispered.

"That's my ex my family **still** invite **to stuff. But I already told her — I'm with whatever."**

And just like that?

She humbled real quick.

Everything was going good until they said they were bringing the baby out.

I'm thinking — okay, maybe a cute baby moment.

But baby, when them fireworks went off, when them dancers came out, when the whole damn backyard went silent for a baby entrance —

I just knew.

They brought him out like a prince.

And when I saw him?

It was **my baby.**

My knees buckled.

My heart dropped.

My baby. My man. My friends.

Nah, this couldn't be real.

I ran.

Couldn't breathe.

My BRISTA found me outside crying, holding me like,

"Friend, what's wrong?"

I could barely speak.

Jessica and Tamika came up tipsy from the bar like,

"Girl, what happened?"

When I told them that was my baby, they looked at me like I was joking.

Jessica was like,

"Wait — true crime much?"

I was like,

"Girl, not now."

She said,

"Well, you gave the baby up, right? You made your choice. Own it."

And she wasn't wrong.

But Tamika made it worse, talkin' 'bout,

"Look at it this way — DJ gon' be bitin' your ass soon anyway."

We all cracked up after that.

And that laugh?

It saved me.

My BRISTA hyped me up:

"You a bad bitch. Walk back in there and tell DJ your truth."

And I did.

Walked back in, head high, crew behind me like a scene out a movie.

I told DJ everything.

And shockingly?

He didn't flip.

He looked at me with the softest eyes and said,

"You wanna meet him up close?"

I said,

"No. Let's just let it be."

And he respected that.

Later that night, we got a text in the group chat.

Tomorrow was Ditch Day.

Carnival time.

I was down — and so was my brother, who was still in town.

What I didn't expect?

My BRISTA and my brother catching eyes and catching feelings.

It was cute, though.

Made me laugh watching them flirt like teenagers.

DJ rented a whole bus for us — me, Jessica, Tamika, my brother, his new lil' boo, everybody.

The carnival was lit.

Until Jessica, being Jessica, was like,

"Let's ditch these boys."

We dipped and ran into some fine dudes from another school.

One of them?

That same boy from the basketball game.

He was like,

"You never hit me up."

I said,

"My bad. Life been **life-ing."**

So we head to their car — Jessica and Tamika in the backseat giggling, and me standing outside talking to Naeem, this smooth-talking charmer who had me forgetting the world for a second.

Then it happened.

Two black cars pull up.

Windows roll down.

Guns out.

Shots fired.

Naeem grabbed me fast.

We ran — me screaming,

"My friends! My friends!"

He said,

"Shut up! We gotta go!"

It was chaos.

Sirens.

Blood.

We found DJ and rushed to the hospital.

Nobody knew who got hit and who made it.

The doctor came out and told us Jessica was okay — it missed her.

But Tamika?

She was in surgery.

Might not make it.

One of Naeem's friends died.

Another in critical condition.

I stormed out, couldn't hold it together.

And like a damn love triangle, here come both my men — DJ and Naeem — chasing behind me.

My brother waved them off like,

"I got her,"

and took me home.

My dad was talkin' my head off, but I was shut down.

Phone off.

Emotions numb.

Days passed.

Jessica finally got through and told me Tamika was recovering.

We went to visit her.

But guess who else was there?

TEE TEE.

Turns out, Tamika and Tee Tee are cousins.

Small-ass world.

Jessica was ready to jump her on sight, but I stopped her.

Tee wanted to talk.

Said she missed me.

Said she was sorry.

And honestly?

I missed my best friend too.

So we squashed it, hugged it out —

but best believe I kept my eye on her.

Later, Naeem called.

Said he wanted to make things right.

He picked me up, took me to a steakhouse, brought flowers, gifts — the whole nine.

But the waitress kept hovering.

I was like,

"Do you know her?"

He said,

"We used to date."

Eye roll.

Dinner ended and when the bill came — his card declined.

I wanted to melt into the floor.

He called his mom — turns out she froze it 'cause she didn't recognize the charge.

Card worked after that, but the waitress?

Salty.

She wanted him to fold, but nah baby — we ate, and we left.

He wanted to go clubbing after, but I had cheer tryouts.

So he kissed me goodbye and dropped me off.

And just like that, the chaos settled.

For now.

Chapter Five

The Baddest – Chapter Five

By Bellami Underwood

The next morning hit me like a reality check.

The whole school knew about the shooting.

I felt exposed. Anxious.

But leave it to Jessica to bring me back to life.

"Girl, fuck these people," she said.

"We got cheer tryouts."

We pulled up like nothing ever happened — well, almost nothing.

Jessica's arm was still in a sling, but baby, that didn't stop her from screaming my name like a proud mama.

The tryouts were wild — ghetto to the max — just my type of crew.

Loud, bold, turnt up.

I made the team, and honestly?

I was hyped.

But that was only half my day.

This school was giving me options and I was taking *full* advantage.

After tryouts, I had an internship at a law firm lined up.

No car yet, so DJ dropped me off.

He kissed my cheek like,

"Go be great," and sped off.

I walked into the building... and whew.

Tall.

Chocolate.

In shape.

My new boss, *Mr. Lawson*, was fine as hell.

I had to stop and ask myself:

Is every man in the South fine or is it just me?

But before I could get carried away, in walked *his wife.*

Mrs. Chanel Lawson.

And baby, when I tell you this woman looked like a runway dream?

Tall. Regal. Confidence in every step.

She introduced herself and her man like they were royalty — and I was just some intern from Philly.

Still, she didn't make me feel small.

She welcomed me in and introduced me to everyone.

My favorite?

A girl named Neva.

She was funny, smart, and showed me all the ropes without making me feel like a rookie.

After finishing up some paperwork, Chanel asked me to step into her office.

She poured a glass of champagne and said,

"Let's talk."

That's when it all changed.

She asked me about my past.

My dreams.

My future.

Then she looked me dead in the eye and said,

"I want to be your fairy *boss* mother."

I laughed, but she didn't.

She was serious.

"I'm going to upgrade your life," she said.

And she did.

Chanel put me in designer.

Took me to a luxury salon.

Paid my first deposit on a new apartment.

She even invited me to a private event later that week.

Now listen — I'm not dumb.

Nobody does all this for nothing.

I knew there had to be a catch.

And I was about to find out.

That night, I pulled up to a huge mansion.

Nervous.

I had Jessica on the phone like,

"Girl, here's my location. If anything go left**, send the feds."**

She was like,

"Girl, you dramatic."

But better safe than sorry.

I walked in, and Chanel greeted me like I was her daughter.

She told me I cleaned up *real* nice.

Introduced me to a group of stunning women and told me,

"These are the Lawson girls."

I said,

"What's a Lawson girl?"

She smiled.

"We speak to high-valued men. They pay us for our time, our conversation... and sometimes more."

I blinked.

"Wait — do we gotta... y'know... sleep with them?"

One girl laughed.

"It's up to you."

I excused myself real quick and hit the bathroom, dialing Jessica in panic.

She screamed,

"Girl, ask them can I do it too!"

I couldn't believe her — but also, it was a smart move.

So I pulled Chanel to the side and told her about my friend.

She agreed to let Jessica come to the next event.

When Jessica arrived?

She looked *so cute* but tried to flex with a fake bag.

Chanel clocked her T *immediately.*

"Babe, we don't do fake," she said, handing her a real one and telling her to tighten up.

Just like that, my girl was in.

And suddenly this life didn't feel so foreign.

That night, one of the girls introduced us to a man named Bennett.

Ugly as sin.

But sweet.

Jessica took the lead and ended up scoring us a trip on his yacht.

All expenses paid.

I didn't think much of it — until I found out it included a private jet and *his friends.*

That's when I met **Mr. 50K**.

Whew.

This man had a presence.

Calm. Confident. Classy.

Turns out?

He was royalty.

An African prince — or maybe even a king.

He told me about his family, his culture, and said he could tell I was different.

"Different how?" I asked.

He nodded toward Jessica.

"Look at her and look at you. You're just caught up. But I see the real you."

He said he wanted to help me change my life.

I asked him how.

He smiled and said,

"Money fixes a lot."

I laughed.

Until my phone buzzed.

Bank alert: $50,000 wired from Mr. 50K.

I damn near dropped my drink.

He said,

"That's just to show you what real men do."

Jessica was living it up.

DJ was nowhere in sight.

Tamika was still recovering.

My BRISTA?

Now my brother-in-law.

And me?

I was walking off a luxury yacht, holding $50K in my account, heading to dinner with a king.

But reality was knocking.

I had cheer practice in the morning.

I had work.

I had a *life.*

I couldn't stay.

He booked my flight.

Sent me off like a gentleman.

But when I got on the plane...

I realized I forgot my man's number.

Not *Mr. 50K.*

My actual man. DJ.

How the hell do you forget your man's number?

But I had a plan.

And trust me —

it was ***the* plan.**

Chapter Six

The Baddest – Chapter Six

By Bellami Underwood

The next day, I needed to link with Jessica.

She texted me that her night was amazing and she'd be home soon, but in the meantime, I had to get my own shit in order.

I had cheer practice, texts from Naeem, missed calls from DJ, and I still needed to get Mr. 50K's number back from Jess.

Too many men.

Not enough time.

Only for me to open my phone and see *him.*

My ex.

My first heartbreak.

Kev.

Sir, why are you confessing your love to me on social media like we forgot what you did?

You think sending me voice notes about "missing me" gonna erase the past?

Ignored. Blocked. Next.

I pulled up to practice with the cheer team — *Critical Damage* — and baby, they weren't playing.

The captain, cocky-ass Ceee?

Light-skinned, built like a video vixen, and rude as hell.

I wasn't tryna get on her bad side, so I kept my energy cute and my moves sharp.

I learned some new steps, hit every count, and stayed in formation.

After practice, I rushed home to change.

Jess told me to meet her at her job — some upscale lounge where she bartended at night.

But first, I had to patch things up with DJ.

He'd been blowing up my phone, but I could feel he was pulling away.

So I called him and we agreed to meet up at his favorite spot — chicken and waffles.

Of course, I overslept and was late.

He was irritated.

We sat down and talked.

Well — we *tried* to talk.

Every two seconds, this loud-ass waitress kept interrupting us.

I'm like,

"Can you back up and refill my cup instead of blowing up my date?"

DJ, with his usual slick mouth, hit me with:

"I'm cool with us just talking. I'm talking to other people too."

Record scratch.

Excuse me?

Boy, don't play with me.

I will slap you, your mama, *and* the syrup off this table.

So I did what any real one would —

I caused a scene.

Arguing with him *and* the waitress because nah.

Not too much on me.

He eventually calmed me down — and that's why I love him.

He knows how to handle my storm.

But we still got kicked out the restaurant.

As we stood outside, I told him I had to go see Jessica at her job and asked if he wanted to come.

He hit me with the:

"Nah, I'm good."

Still salty.

Whatever.

I headed to Jess's job, and something felt off.

She didn't look like herself.

She leaned in and said,

"Girl, I tested positive for an STD... and I'm pregnant."

I froze.

"What?! By who??"

She shrugged,

"I don't even know."

I damn near flipped the bar over.

"Did you handle it?"

She nodded,

"Yeah. I'm good now."

We sat and talked about our wild nights.

I finally got Mr. 50K's number and texted him immediately.

No response.

I said,

"Oop — maybe he's over me already."

While I'm sipping on a drink, this girl walks up — *Quay with the four Y's.*

Loud, flashy, and fine.

She ordered bottles from Jess and invited me to her section, which was packed with NFL and NBA players.

You know I went.

Quay was cool, though.

Real chill.

She asked me,

"You **know any of the Chargers that just won the Super Bowl?"**

I did.

But I wasn't tryna come off like a groupie.

Then came Melvin.

The quarterback.

And baby, he was looking at me like I was *the trophy.*

He asked Quay if he could talk to me and slid over like,

"Take my number."

I smirked,

"Nah, you take mine."

Later, I told Jess I was heading out.

I had a test to study for and shifts to pick up.

I went home, reset, and went to work the next day.

While chatting with Chanel, I told her about everything.

Her response?

"I know."

I said,

"What?"

"I know you got 50K. I know what Jess got too. I set it all up."

My jaw dropped.

This woman knew everything.

She said,

"You got 50K, I got 100K. Now after work, I need you to do something for me."

She handed me an address and told me to deliver a package.

Cool.

I went home, got dressed, and dropped it off at a hotel.

Guess who opened the door?

Melvin.

He said,

"You **one of her girls?"**

I blinked.

"Excuse me?"

"If not, why are you dropping off her stuff?"

I brushed him off.

"Mind your business."

Back in the car, I was heated.

Called Chanel like,

"Girl, did you set this up too?"

Her response?

"Mmmhm."

This woman is two steps ahead of everybody.

Later that night, I met up with Melvin again for our little aquarium date.

He was sweet.

But also boring as hell.

Talked about fish for twenty minutes straight like we was on Animal Planet.

Whole time I'm thinking,

Sir, shut up.

But still...

It was cute.

Chapter Seven

The Baddest – Chapter Seven

By Bellami Underwood

Meanwhile, the date kept dragging on.

I tried to stay present, but my mind?

It was still stuck on DJ.

He kept blowing up my phone, texting

"wyd?" and

"how's **everything?"**

like every five minutes.

Sir, mind your damn business.

I hit "decline," threw him on Do Not Disturb, and finally focused on my plate.

Melvin, though?

He was a good dude... but damn, he talked too much.

I kept thinking — maybe I shouldn't have even come out tonight.

Multitasking under the table, I texted DJ real quick:

"I'm sorry. We'll talk soon."

Then I opened up social media to kill time — and boom.

Kev.

My ex.

Blowing me up from a fake page, talking about:

"I'll be in town soon."

Sir, **leave me the fuck alone.**

In my head, I was already planning to be **nowhere he could find me.**

Melvin kept asking,

"You good? Everything okay?"

I fake-smiled,

"Yeah... can we just finish the date?"

I already knew then:

He wouldn't be seeing me again.

Snoozefest athlete. No spark.

The next morning, back at school, Jessica was still in my ear.

Still talking about the STD drama, piecing together every detail like she was a detective.

But me?

Girl, I had my own shit to worry about.

I brushed her off, packed up for cheer practice, and tried to thug it out...

But my stomach wasn't letting up.

In the middle of class, I had to excuse myself and go straight to the women's center.

They asked a bunch of questions, checked me out...

Then told me I needed to go to urgent care.

"We can't figure it out here."

At urgent care, they hit me with the news:

I had an STD.

I damn near hit the floor.

HOW??

Only person I had been with was my baby dad...

And it had been months since.

They weren't interested in the *why*.

They just gave me paperwork and said:

"Contact everybody you've been with."

Everybody?

There wasn't no "everybody."

It was him.

And even though I hated his guts, I did the responsible thing —
Reached out to the few people I needed to.
During that, I ended up talking to my brother —
And he told me something even worse.
He had just tested positive for HIV.
And he said...
"It could've possibly traced **back to your baby dad."**
When I tell you I couldn't breathe?
My mind went straight to my baby —
The one living with DJ's family.
I knew I had to tell DJ immediately.
I called DJ, voice shaking, and told him everything.
He rushed me to his family's house —
But trying to explain myself to them?
A waste of time.
The way they looked at me —
Like I was dirty.
Like I was trash.
"You gave up your rights when you gave him up," they said.
"You need to remove yourself."
They didn't even let me hold my own baby.
DJ tried to calm me down outside, but I was sick to my stomach.
Later, I went to work and vented to Ms. Lawson.
She hugged me and told me everything would be okay —
But even *she* couldn't promise that.
Because no matter how powerful she was,
they had power too.
And they weren't about to back down.
That cut deep.
That night, DJ called me back:
"The baby's okay... but they don't want you around no more."
I told him,
"Stay close. Find out what they planning."

He agreed.

Not even 24 hours later, DJ found out:

They were thinking about giving the baby up.

"We don't do messy."

And to them?

I was messy.

Hearing that flipped a switch in me.

I wasn't about to sit back and watch my baby get passed around like paperwork.

I popped up at they house.

Soon as the mama opened the door?

I let her *have it.*

Security came fast, snatched me up, and threw me off the property like I was nobody.

Sitting on the curb, crying and mad, I called Jessica.

We weren't about to take this laying down.

We made a plan.

Jessica would go to their house the next day,

All smiles like she was just "checking in."

While she distracted them?

I would sneak in to see my baby.

The next day, Brista drove us.

Jessica went inside first, playing her role.

I hopped the gate and slipped into the baby's room.

Soon as he saw me,

He lit up.

My baby knew me.

He still loved me.

I was holding him, trying not to cry, when I heard footsteps.

The nanny was coming.

I panicked and climbed out the window onto the ledge, texting Jessica fast:

"Get the nanny away from the room!"

Jessica got her to go outside, pretending she needed help unloading bags.

I was about to climb back inside when —

The nanny came back in.

And my baby was gone.

OMFG.

Where was he?!

My heart dropped.

Jessica texted:

"Did you leave with him??"

"NO!" I texted back, panicking.

"CALL THE COPS!"

Within minutes, security, cops — everybody was flooding the property.

I made my exit quiet and called DJ.

"Where you **at?"**

"Home. Why?"

Come to find out —

DJ had come home early and scooped up the baby.

Had him safe in his room the whole time.

Thank God.

DJ met us at the front gate and smoothed it over before it got messier.

Later that evening, Ms. Lawson called:

"Come to work. Now."

Me and Jessica pulled up quick.

First thing we saw?

Neva.

Jessica and Neva?

Could not stand each other.

I mediated it quick — we had bigger shit to focus on.

Ms. Lawson sat us down and dropped a bomb:

"Are you ladies ready for a world tour?"

We all screamed:

"YES!"

First stop: New York.

Next up: Philly.

I was lowkey over it — didn't feel like traveling —

But the girls hyped me up until I said yeah.

Ms. Lawson made it clear:

"You're going to meet billionaires. You need to secure $500,000 in deals. No games."

After the meeting, I dipped out and called Mr. 50.

He answered, confused:

"How you **get this number?"**

I smoothed it over, told him I was coming to New York and wanted to see him.

Just like that, he arranged for us to fly on his private jet.

Takeoff was rough —

Turbulence had me praying —

But once we touched down, I felt it:

The Georgia peach was peeling away.

The hustler in me was fully waking up.

Chapter Eight

The Baddest – Chapter Eight

By Bellami Underwood

Touchdown in New York was **not** cute.

Neva and Jessica were still gagging from that plane ride —

Turbulence tossing us around like rag dolls, drinks flying, wigs shifting.

It was a whole mess.

We rushed off the jet, stumbling over each other, just trying to breathe fresh air.

But what made me stop cold?

Ms. Lawson.

Standing at the gate. Waiting for us.

Draped in a cream trench coat, sunglasses on at night, arms crossed.

I blinked.

"Ms. Lawson? What you **doing here?"**

Neva whispered,

"Damn, she don't **trust us?"**

Ms. Lawson just smiled that knowing smile.

"Something told me to hop on the jet and check in personally."

Something in her voice told me it wasn't just a "feeling."

But whatever — we was here now.

She led us to a sleek black SUV waiting outside.

Destination?

Her private townhouse in the Upper East Side.

Baby, when I say luxury?

That woman lived like she printed money.

Soon as we walked in, it was like we hit a jackpot.

Rooms full of designer clothes, glittering jewelry, limited-edition bags, and stacks — **literal stacks** — of cash laid out neatly in boxes like souvenirs.

Ms. Lawson clapped her hands once.

"Pick what you need. And..."

She paused dramatically.

"...for your hard work, here's a bonus."

She handed each of us a thick envelope.

I peeked inside.

Thirty thousand dollars.

I smiled politely, but deep down?

It didn't feel right.

I mean, yeah — I earned it. We worked for it.

But the more she gave, the deeper we were in her pocket.

And I wasn't trying to be nobody's pawn forever.

Plan your next move, Indy. Don't get trapped.

We got dressed for the night — all black everything.

I slipped into a tight lace dress and strapped on my eight-inch stilettos like armor.

Jessica wore a black silk mini.

Neva rocked a body-hugging catsuit that had every curve on display.

When we hit *Greenway Nightclub*?

Heads turned.

We were the moment.

Inside the VIP, the setup was even crazier.

Bottles lined the tables, gold couches, neon lights bouncing off diamond chains.

Men everywhere — suits, sneakers, gold watches — scouting us like prey.

Neva got pulled aside by some slick-talking guy promising "the world."

Me and Jessica worked the room, mingling, sipping champagne, soaking up attention but staying **sharp**.

After a while, I noticed Neva had been gone too long.

Way too long.

Jessica nudged me.

"You **seen Neva?"**

I shook my head.

Something felt **off.**

We pushed through the crowd, made our way to the private back rooms.

When we finally found her?

Neva was slumped on a velvet couch —

Eyes half-closed.

Barely breathing.

"Neva!" Jessica screamed.

I grabbed my phone, dialing Ms. Lawson with shaking hands.

"Emergency. Now."

Security rushed in like a SWAT team.

We wrapped Neva up and rushed her toward the exit, trying to stay lowkey.

As we loaded her into the SUV, I noticed something chilling:

Mr. 50K was watching from across the street.

And someone else... was watching him.

I felt my phone vibrate.

Kev.

I hesitated, then answered.

His voice was low. Mocking.

"You got cars following you, Indy. Make the wrong move and it's gonna be fireworks."

I hung up mid-sentence and alerted security immediately.

But by the time we reached the hospital?

It was too late.

Three blacked-out SUVs cornered us at the ER entrance.

Men jumped out, faces masked, guns flashing under their coats.

One yelled:

"Bring her out — or everybody gets it!"

Without thinking, I bolted from the car, running toward the hospital doors like my life depended on it.

Behind me, I heard Jessica scream —

And when I looked back?

They had snatched her.

My heart stopped.

I ducked behind a pillar inside the ER, watching helplessly as security and Kev's men brawled outside.

Sirens wailed in the distance.

More security swarmed in.

Shots rang out — quick, sharp, brutal.

By the time the smoke cleared?

Kev was gone.

Jessica was gone.

Neva was unconscious in the hospital bed.

And I was standing in the middle of chaos — again.

My phone rang.

Kev.

His voice was smug:

"If you wanna see your little friend again, you know what to do. Come home, baby."

I gripped the phone so hard my knuckles turned white.

Ms. Lawson pulled up minutes later, stepping out the car calm
like **nothing** had just popped off.

I ran up to her, breathless, shaking.

"Kev got Jessica! He said—"

She cut me off with a sharp wave of her hand.

"Don't worry. He don't know who he fucking with. He'll learn."

Her voice was ice cold.

I nodded, swallowing the fear rising in my throat.

Because the truth was?

I knew what was coming next.

I had to go back to Philly.

And this time?

It was personal.

Chapter Nine

The Baddest – Chapter Nine

By Bellami Underwood

Could you imagine?

The baddest bitch —
The one who left Philly broke and heartbroken —
Turning into a *sad bitch...*
Only to come back badder than ever.
Now I was back —
Not the little girl they remembered —
But the queen they wasn't ready for.
But first?
I needed a bed. And some peace.
I checked into a little hotel on the edge of the city,
Threw my bags down, and collapsed face-first into the mattress.
After everything I'd been through —
New York, the club drama, Jessica getting kidnapped —
My body was **begging** for sleep.
Hours later, the sun beaming through cheap curtains woke me up.
I rolled over, stared at the cracked ceiling, and said to myself:
"It's time to turn this city the fuck up."
I hopped out the bed, jumped fresh, and grabbed my phone.
First call?

Tee.

Yeah, that *Tee.*

The same old bestie who snaked me back in the day.

But right now?

I needed someone who knew these Philly streets better than Kev did.

When Tee answered, she sounded shocked.

"Indy?! Girl, what the fuck?!"

"Meet me at Frankford Terminal," I said, voice cold.

"We got work to do."

I slid into the terminal like a shadow.

Black hoodie up.

Sunglasses on.

Tee was already there —

Perched on a bench like she was waiting for a bus to the past.

We locked eyes.

It was weird —

Anger. Betrayal. Loyalty.

All floating between us.

But fuck it.

Bigger shit was at stake.

We dapped up quick and slid into a corner.

I broke it down for her —

Everything.

Kev.

Jessica.

The setup.

Tee shook her head, laughing low.

"Girl, you really got your ass into some shit."

I smirked.

"Ain't that why you always loved me?"

We grabbed breakfast sandwiches from the dirty-ass corner store,

Grease dripping onto napkins, and sat outside planning.

The play was simple:

Tee would call Kev, pretend she hated me,

And act like she was ready to "hand me over."

She pulled out a burner phone, dialing fast.

Kev picked up on the first ring.

"Yo," he barked.

Tee flipped into her old grimy self instantly.

"I know where Indy at. **She back in Philly, sloppy as fuck. I can line** her for **you."**

Kev paused.

"Bet. Where?"

They arranged a meet-up at an old, abandoned garage everybody called *The Hideaway.*

Perfect.

But before the meet?

I had one more mission:

My mom's house.

Big mistake.

When she opened the door,

She stared at me like I was trash blowing down the block.

Still mad.

Still bitter.

Still stuck.

We got into it immediately.

Old wounds. Old arguments.

"You abandoned your family!" she snapped.

"You never loved me!" I shouted back.

The yelling shook the whole damn block.

But when I pulled out a wad of cash and slapped **$10,000** into her hand?

Silence.

Money still ran **this city.**

She let me inside, showed me the half-assed renovations she tried to do on the house,

Bragging like she built the Taj Mahal.

I barely listened.

I had bigger things to handle.

I called my baby dad — *Daul* —

Told him pull up outside.

When he rolled up, he looked the same:

Dirty hoodie. Lying eyes.

I leaned against his car, folded my arms.

"You gave me an STD," I said bluntly.

"You lied about everything."

"You ain't shit."

He mumbled some bullshit about "healing" and "truth,"

But I wasn't trying to hear none of it.

So I snatched my water bottle from my bag and splashed it dead in his face.

"Fuck you, pussy."

He gasped, wiping his eyes, looking stupid as hell while I strutted back into my mom's house.

Closure served cold.

I texted Tee:

"You ready?"

She was.

But what Tee didn't know?

I had already called Ms. Lawson too —

Told her *everything.*

And Ms. Lawson?

She was on her way.

With backup.

The Hideaway looked like something out of a horror movie.

Broken windows. Graffiti everywhere.

Cold air leaking out the cracks.

I pulled up first in a black truck, parked in the shadows.

Then Kev arrived, his own SUV pulling up slow, headlights off.

And what I saw through the windshield?

Jessica.

Tied up.

Mouth taped shut.

Eyes wide and terrified.

My heart clenched.

Kev hopped out, swaggering like he owned the night.

"All this for what, Kev?" I yelled across the lot.

He just smirked — that sick, twisted smirk I remembered too well —

And stalked toward me.

"I miss you," he said low.

Before I could move, he grabbed my face and kissed me —

Rough. Desperate.

I jerked back, disgusted.

But then I had an idea.

Play along. Stall him.

So I kissed him back — soft, slow —

Just enough to make him think he was winning.

Then?

I hauled off and kicked him dead in his nuts.

Kev screamed, doubling over.

I swung at him, fists flying, but he was too strong.

He tackled me, wrestling me toward his truck,

Shoving me into the passenger seat.

Just as he slammed the door shut—

Headlights.

Engines roaring.

Twenty black trucks circling **the lot.**

Ms. Lawson had arrived.

Fifty men jumped out, **guns drawn.**

Ms. Lawson herself stepping out in heels, fur coat blowing in the wind,

Calm as a *mafia boss.*

She pointed dead at Kev.

"Let my girls go — or you won't make it out this lot alive."

Kev froze.

Within seconds, he crumbled.

Jessica was released first —

Stumbling toward me, crying.

Tee too — hands trembling, but free.

I thought it was over.

But Ms. Lawson wasn't done.

She snapped her fingers.

Two men grabbed Kev.

Two more grabbed Tee.

I spun around.

"Ms. Lawson, what the fuck?!"

She didn't even blink.

"Payback," she said.

She **pistol-whipped Tee** across the face.

Tee dropped like a rock.

Then she turned the gun on Kev —

And **pulled the trigger.**

Blood splattered across the pavement.

Kev dropped, lifeless.

The world tilted.

Screams echoed in my ears.

I covered my mouth,

Heart pounding out my chest.

What had we just done?

What the fuck was I supposed to do now?

Chapter Ten

The Baddest – Chapter Ten

By Bellami Underwood

I was screaming at Ms. Lawson, **begging her to stop.**

My voice cracked, raw with panic.

Jessica grabbed my arm and yanked me back.

"Let it go," she whispered, her voice tight.

"He deserves it, Indy. You saw what he did. He kidnapped me. He could've killed me."

Ms. Lawson and her men bagged Kev and Tee like they was trash —

Duct-taping their hands, throwing them into the back of a blacked-out truck.

Then she turned to me, tossing me a cold glance.

"You coming **too."**

No choice.

Me, Jessica, and Ms. Lawson climbed into another car,

Following the caravan deep into the city.

The streets blurred past — neon lights flickering like dying stars.

Halfway through the ride, my phone buzzed.

Neva.

She sounded weak but determined.

"I'm feeling better," she said.

"I'll meet y'all back in Philly."

When we finally arrived at the "secure location" —

Some abandoned warehouse on the edge of the city —

Neva was already there.

While the men dragged Kev and Tee inside,

Me and Jessica huddled near the entrance.

I turned to her, my stomach twisting in guilt.

"This is going too far," I said, voice shaking.

"I just wanted you back, Jess. I never wanted nobody dead."

Jessica frowned, confused.

"Indy... what you **mean?"**

I swallowed hard.

"I never told you," I whispered.

"Before I left Philly... I was dealing with Kev *and* my baby dad."

Her mouth dropped open.

"What the fuck?"

"And... Kev thought the baby could've been his."

Jessica stared at me, stunned silent.

We pulled Ms. Lawson aside to tell her everything, hoping she'd show mercy.

When we finished explaining, Ms. Lawson threw her head back and laughed.

"Baby girl," she said,

"I don't care if Kev was your baby daddy, your real daddy, or Jesus Christ himself."

She snapped her fingers.

"I ain't gon' kill him no more. I'm just gon' make him my bitch."

"And Tee?" Ms. Lawson added, smirking.

"I'll let her go — if she agrees to work for me."

Tee, tied up on the floor, nodded frantically without hesitation.

While the dust settled, my phone lit up again.

DJ.

I answered immediately.

"Indy, you gotta get back. NOW. They're giving the baby up in a few hours!"

My vision blurred.

"What?! NO!"

Jessica and Neva turned toward me, alarmed.

I turned to Ms. Lawson, desperate.

"I need to go! Please! Let me take the jet!"

Ms. Lawson shook her head.

"Jet's getting repaired. Storm damage."

Without thinking, I booked the first commercial flight I could find.

Traffic was hell.

I was banging my fists on the car window, begging every light to turn green.

At the airport, I was running —

Pushing past people, screaming at security to let me through.

Tears streaked my face. People stared.

I didn't care.

I needed my baby.

I barely made it to the gate before they closed it.

On the plane, I sobbed quietly into my hoodie.

They had no idea what was at stake.

The flight dragged.

By the time we touched down in Georgia, it was already dark.

DJ was waiting outside the terminal, engine running, eyes wild.

I jumped in the car.

"We're almost there," he kept saying.

I stared out the window,

Praying harder than I ever prayed in my life.

When we pulled into his parents' driveway, the house was dark.

No cars. No lights.

Something was wrong.

DJ sprinted to the door, banging.

No answer.

Finally, the door creaked open —

And his mama stood there, arms crossed, face blank.

DJ pushed past her, calling out for the baby.

Room after room — **empty.**

Crib — **empty.**

Toys — **gone.**

Finally, his mama spoke:

"He's gone."

Just like that.

Gone.

I fell to my knees.

The scream ripping from my chest so loud,

It shook the whole damn house.

Gone.

My baby was gone.

And I had no idea

Where to even start looking.

Acknowledgments

By Bellami Underwood

To every **Brista** who picked this book up,

Pressed play on a voice memo,

Watched the series,

Or shared a clip —

This is for you.

To the survivors, the storytellers, the secret-keepers, and the soft-hearted soldiers —

Thank you for loving me through **every version of myself.**

You made *The Baddest* real.

You made *me* real.

Forever grateful,

Bellami

Stay Connected

baddestbook.com

Follow @bellamiuw on all platforms for:

• Behind-the-scenes stories

• Exclusive visuals and cast reveals

• Book Two teasers & drop dates

Join the BRISTA Family and get early access to:

• Preorders

- **Launch updates**
- **VIP-only content**

About the Author

Bellami Underwood is a powerhouse storyteller and content creator, born in Hawai'i and raised in Frankford, Philadelphia.

Known for his raw storytimes and viral presence, Bellami brings truth, trauma, and brilliance to every project. From podcast clips to unforgettable videos to his debut novel, *The Baddest*, Bellami is building a media empire rooted in Black queer storytelling and survivor spirit.

Follow Bellami: @bellamiuw

Coming Soon – Book Two

Preview: The Baddest – Book Two

Ms. Lawson is gone — vanished into shadows, **leaving the government scrambling to track her down.**

Indyanna?

She's locked up.

The charges? Sealed.

The truth? Buried beneath loyalty and blood.

She still doesn't know who her baby's father is.

And her baby? Missing.

Jessica is on the run, ducking the police and dodging betrayals.

DJ's family is unraveling, blaming him for a storm he didn't start.

And Kev?

He's coming to Georgia.

This time, nobody's playing nice.

And *The Baddest* is about to become...

The Most Wanted.

Chapter 13

Chapter 14

Chapter 15

Chapter 16

Chapter 17

Chapter 18

Chapter 19

Chapter 20

Chapter 21

Made in the USA
Columbia, SC
05 June 2025

1d9e9485-49e5-43dd-9b50-9f61b5d94ce4R01